The Secret in
Miranda's Closet

The Secret in Miranda's Closet

Written and illustrated by

SHEILA GREENWALD

A Yearling Book

Published by
Dell Publishing
a division of
The Bantam Doubleday Dell Publishing Group, Inc.
666 Fifth Avenue
New York, New York 10103

ISBN: 0-440-40128-3

Printed in the United States of America

January 1989

10 9 8 7 6 5 4 3 2 1

CW

To my mother

1

The moment Miranda saw the doll lying at the bottom of a chest of table linen she thought she was the loveliest she'd ever seen. Even stuffed between two stacks of dinner napkins, the doll appeared graceful and charming, as if she were resting for a moment and had not been left some fifty years before in a box in an attic and apparently forgotten. Miranda picked her up carefully. Her bisque face was fresh and serene. Her dress was a somewhat faded calico and her high-heeled bisque shoes and ankles protruded daintily from mesh pantaloons. Miranda placed her on top of the chest and stood back to admire

1

her. She was a beauty. No question about
it. Lovely dark blue eyes of extraordinarily
deep glass, dimpled chin, graceful neck,
high round bosom, tiny waist, delicate
bisque fingers. A perfect miniature wonder. Miranda was lost in pleasure at the
good fortune of finding her. She couldn't
wait to learn her history. She was sure the
doll had belonged to someone a very long
time ago, someone who had left her care-
lessly in the linen chest and forgotten her.
Miranda couldn't think of Mrs. Nesbit as
ever having been interested in dolls. It

must have been Mrs. Nesbit's mother or perhaps her grandmother.

She held the doll between the fingers of one hand and carefully felt her way down the steep attic steps. These steps ended up curiously in a closet off the kitchen. As Miranda started to descend the last flight, she heard her name being spoken by Mrs. Nesbit. Miranda turned prickly and cold. It was odd hearing somebody talking about you, odd and alarming and fascinating. Her mother said no one ever said anything good, either, but Miranda simply sat herself down to listen.

"The awful thing about it," Mrs. Nesbit was saying, "is that everyone takes it out on Miranda, and of course it's not her fault. It isn't Miranda's fault that her charming mum drops her, plunk, at a moment's notice, on someone's doorstep for a weekend. Naturally everyone feels taken advantage of and it's the poor Lump who gets the brunt of it, never her outrageous, delicious mother. Ah, well, life is not fair and Olivia clearly has not had all the breaks."

"How does the child take it?" another voice said.

"Miranda? Who knows. She's not exactly a communicative little beast. I can't, however, think it's easy for her to be the plunked party. Also, I'm sure Olivia was lying, telling me she's got heaps of work to get through and a deadline and couldn't possibly have the child at home. The child is quiet as a mouse, and when I called Olivia in the city before there was no answer. Obviously she popped the kid on one bus at the terminal and took herself off on another for a weekend someplace with her flame of the moment. I'm quite certain the Lump knows all about it."

"The Lump knows all sorts of secret bits about the mysterious Olivia, I'll bet," said the other voice, "and she's learned to keep her lips buttoned."

Miranda held the doll to her and rocked it. She closed her eyes and tried not to feel the huge iron weight that slid down her throat and was dragging everything inside her sickeningly down. She wanted to run

away, to get off the stuffy, musty steps, but she couldn't move. If she could, it was back to the attic, for she could never go through the door into the kitchen. NEVER.

The voices were relentless. "Hasn't she any school friends to stay with? Surely there should be somebody other than you, Audrey. Somebody younger and nearer."

"School friends?" Mrs. Nesbit laughed. "Have you seen her? She is your classic miserable child. She's that sad, sullen, little troll we all remember who sat at the back of the classroom for years and who nobody ever cared to know." There was the sound of the kettle boiling through a whistle and then of china and table silver.

"Well, this is my weekend to be stuck with her, so I'd best stop complaining and try to treat her tolerably," Audrey Nesbit said with a full mouth.

"Perhaps I could help you out. She could come to town with me and amuse herself at the drugstore while I shop."

"She's amusing herself in my attic, dear, and I would expect that to last for a few more hours. There's tons of old trash up there. Then we'll have lunch. She can watch TV or go play outdoors if it snows. Actually, she's not at all difficult, and it isn't her fault."

"It's Olivia's."

"But everybody *loves* Olivia," Audrey said sarcastically.

"Everybody's afraid of Olivia might be stating it more honestly," said the other woman. "I for one would hate to have her for an enemy. The only thing to do is sit tight."

"And sit for the Lump."

The two women chuckled. There were sounds of chairs scraping.

Miranda Alexis (sometimes known as the Lump or the Blimp) Perry got up as noiselessly as possible and climbed back up to the attic. She sat down on a partially unraveled rattan chair and took off her glasses, which were steamy from perspiration. She put the doll on her knee. Her heart was still banging from the climb, the job of being a quiet spy, and the awful things she had just heard. She looked at the doll and wished fervently that they could change places. Miranda knew perfectly well that such things were not possible, but knowing that didn't prevent her from wishing to be the delicate pink and white bisque figure in a full calico skirt.

"If I were you," she said out loud to the doll, "I would go downstairs and tell Mrs. Audrey Nesbit that I hate being here as much as she hates having me, that I have had it with being plunked, and that Olivia is *not* charming, she's . . ." Miranda stopped. She couldn't think of an appropriate word. "She keeps putting me places where I don't want to be as if I were a baby who couldn't take care of herself which I can which she doesn't know because she's too busy to find out. Also, she *is* off for the weekend and his name is Alistair and he's a *drip*. A drip in tweed with leather patches even if he is head of Olivia's department at the university, and though I do in fact sit in the last seat at school and don't make friends, I think a lot of thoughts and one of them is how I HATE PEOPLE LIKE AUDREY NESBIT AND I HATE BEING IN THEIR HOUSES TRYING NOT TO BE A NUISANCE AND I HATE SITTING IN THEIR ATTICS PRETENDING I HAVEN'T HEARD THINGS."

This outburst helped Miranda calm down. She picked the doll up again, dusted herself off, and went downstairs. When she reached the bottom landing she listened long enough to find out if she was still being discussed. She wasn't. The conversation had changed. And something else had changed. Up in the attic Miranda Alexis Perry had changed, not into an antique bisque doll, but into a person a few people were going to know about in the months to come.

2

"Oh, Miranda." Mrs. Nesbit looked worried. "Did you just come down?" She exchanged a nervous glance with the other woman in the kitchen, a tall, thin lady in a tan pantsuit.

"No," said Miranda. "I was sitting on the steps for a little while." She gazed as blandly as she could at the two women. "Why?"

"No reason." Mrs. Nesbit bent her frizzy head and moved her coffee cup around. Miranda fully enjoyed the uncomfortable silence.

"What can you tell me about this doll?" Miranda produced the little figure from behind her back.

"Why, for heaven's sake." Mrs. Nesbit smiled with relief. "She was mine for a short while — very short, I couldn't stand dolls. But she was my mother's and before that my Aunt Katie's. She's called Dinah and she has or had at one time an immense and enviable wardrobe of every imaginable costume. A steamer trunk crammed with ball gowns, travel suits, riding habits, nighties, corsets, petticoats, and even a little jewel case with tiny chokers, rings, and bracelets."

Miranda's imagination soared. She couldn't remember ever being so excited. Suddenly she saw this lovely Dinah in her elegant clothes in a beautiful world made out of bits and pieces she remembered from books and movies. She completely forgot all the awful things she had heard only a short time before in that same kitchen.

"Do you play with *dolls,* Miranda?" the lady in the pantsuit, a Ms. Dryden, was asking.

"Olivia's daughter play with dolls? You

must be mad." Mrs. Nesbit laughed. "Your mother doesn't let you play with dolls, does she, Miranda?"

Miranda knew that her mother was being made fun of and didn't like it.

"I have had a few," she answered stonily. "They didn't amuse me. However, this one is interesting because it's old. I would like to see her clothes, what sort of thing they made for dolls in those days."

Again the two ladies exchanged glances. "Okay, Miranda," Mrs. Nesbit said. "See if you can locate a large blue-and-white-striped hatbox with a violet ribbon around it up in the attic. Inside, if I recall, there's a perfect little steamer trunk stuffed with clothes. Feast your eyes."

Miranda tried not to show her almost unbearable delight. Keeping her face blank, she thanked Mrs. Nesbit and went back up to the attic. "Olivia would have a fit," she heard along with a whoop of laughter from the kitchen.

Olivia. Tall, slender, flaming red–haired, green-eyed Olivia Perry, sociologist, critic, and editor. While she inspired fear, respect, outrage, and amusement in the two ladies in the kitchen, she inspired other things in her daughter Miranda. Loyalty and pride were the good things, the rest Miranda didn't like to think about. She puffed a bit as she got to the top bank of stairs. She really was a lump and climbing stairs wasn't easy.

She had begun to know a while ago (she couldn't remember exactly when) that she was not at all the proper daughter for Olivia Perry. Olivia should have had a very different sort of girl, and Miranda even knew who this girl should have been. Townsend (or Towny) Ordway, that's who. Towny, Alistair's daughter, was a beanpole with thick honey-colored hair worn in a long ponytail that she flicked artfully from one side of her neck to the other. Miranda believed that Towny had the breezy, cool style of a popular girl. "Hi, I'm Towny," she could say with no trouble. "Don't think we've met."

It sounded so easy if you knew how. Miranda didn't know how and never would. Even her questions to Audrey Nesbit were unusual for Miranda. She had broken one of her rules, which was never to begin a conversation. She had only done so today because of Dinah.

On the floor under a dusty pile of old *Harper's Monthly*s was the blue hatbox. Its ribbon, a faded sateen bow, fell away. Miranda withdrew the cracked cover and sighed with pleasure. There was the steamer trunk. She opened it and pulled out its drawers. Carefully folded in green tissue paper or hanging from tiny hangers was Dinah's wardrobe. One by one Miranda removed the contents of the trunk. One by one she marveled at their detail and delicacy until she came upon the last dress, a filmy tea gown with a pale flower design, floaty sleeves, and a velvet sash. Beneath the gown lay a small printed card bordered with daisies. On it was written: "Miss Dinah, Please to attend a Garden Party in the Garden at Noon on Sunday."

Miranda looked into the space of the

window, where snowflakes could be seen falling gently. A garden party, however, was what she saw. The garden had green lawns and hedges and white wrought-iron benches and statues and fountains and the lovely Dinah in her sweet dress, a glass of something icy in one hand, a parasol in the other.

"By all means I shall dress you for the party," Miranda said out loud. "You couldn't miss it for all the world."

And that was how Miranda Alexis (sometimes known as the Lump or the Blimp) Perry embarked upon an unusual game with a doll named Dinah that would bring her pleasure and hurt and anger and would change her life forever after.

3

First she went to the upstairs bathroom and washed her hands thoroughly. Then she returned to the attic. She looked at Dinah and the pile of clothes and her heart sank. It was so dirty up there. Dinah shouldn't be in such a place. But to take her downstairs would place the game in jeopardy, and Miranda knew the game had to be private to the point of secrecy.

She dressed Dinah with care in the floaty mauve gown and selected a picture hat with a silk ribbon to tie under her chin. The snowflakes now fell thickly outside the attic window, which cast a pale gray light, but for Miranda the garden she made out of an arrangement of boxes was lush and green. Dinah moved here and there among the benches and fountains with a grace and charm that could captivate whole armies.

"How do you do, I am Dinah Lovelace and I am new in this neighborhood. Lord Blessington, heavens no, I don't believe we have ever met." Dinah was excellent at enduring snubs and telling people off so they hardly knew it. Dinah was a combination of all the heroines Miranda had loved and possessed all the qualities she admired. Dinah always knew the right thing to say. Although she was the daughter of a poor carpenter she could charm old Lord Blessington, and *even* the snobbish Duchess of Dilby was impressed by her wit and good humor.

Miranda moved the doll around her assemblage of boxes and spoke for her, creating her own world full of characters. And the snow fell and the hours passed.

"Miranda, are you still up there?" Mrs. Nesbit's voice rang up the stairway, breaking into the ongoing drama.

Quickly and guiltily Miranda gathered up the scattered boxes.

"Well, for heaven's sake." Audrey Nesbit was trudging up the stairs. "You little gnome." This was a new one to Miranda. "I couldn't imagine where you were hiding. There's about a foot of snow gathered outside and it's still coming down. Do you want some lunch?" Her face appeared in the door.

Miranda, now a blank, followed Mrs. Nesbit down the musty steps back into the kitchen. Half of the kitchen table was covered with stacks of typing paper, a manuscript, a typewriter, and pencils, half with cold meats and salad and cheese. The kitchen was Audrey Nesbit's study.

"Help yourself, Miranda. Just make a sandwich of what you like, only don't get mayo on my article. I've got a few friends coming in later, snow permitting. We're writers. We read our work out loud and offer criticism and help. I'm sure you'd be bored to tears, so you can watch TV or play in the snow."

"I'm not through looking at Dinah," said Miranda, assembling cheese and bologna on a slab of whole wheat bread.

"Who?"

"Dinah, the doll."

"Oh, of course." Mrs. Nesbit smiled. "Goodness, Miranda, you *are* interested in her, aren't you? What *would* Olivia think?"

Miranda looked her blankest.

"I'm sure if you'd been a boy she'd have given you dozens, but I'll bet for you, Miranda, it was Tonka trucks and model submarines from the beginning."

"I did have lots of trucks," Miranda conceded, "but I also had a family of dolls." She remembered her dreary little doll family. They were so ugly and clumsy that she never played with them. Olivia had been delighted to see her reject them and even wrote an article about it. Miranda heard her tell her friends, "You see, she's not compelled to role play. She has been given a choice and she prefers her gucks." "Gucks" was Miranda's baby word for "trucks." Miranda had offered to give the

19

dolls away. But the doll family that had been hand made by children at an institution Olivia supported inhabited another world than Dinah. They were rustic and brutish where she was delicate and lovely.

Of course Miranda had not had much time at home to play with the dolls or the trucks. Olivia had sent her off to play groups ever since she could remember. Miranda loathed groups. They tired her out. Olivia had always said, "Miranda needs other children." She didn't. She needed to be alone to rest and dream. Though she rarely had the opportunity, Miranda loved being alone and was very good at it. She could fix a meal, clean up, or read a book. She resented being sent to groups like a baby, or having to be baby-sat for by Audrey Nesbit. She could take perfectly good care of herself. But standing up to Olivia's plans was not simple, and it was easier to go along than to object. She knew that Olivia was frequently annoyed with her lack of enthusiasm and wished she would cooperate. There were times when Olivia was terrific, when they were like room-mates, sharing thoughts and experiences and enjoying each other, but then she would get busy and distracted and shove Miranda off to another horrible group, giving her all kinds of reasons why she should love it. Life with Olivia was confusing.

Now she assembled meats and cheese and slathered a thick layer of mayonnaise on her bread and bit in and filled her cheeks.

"My, but that's a nice fat sandwich you've made," Mrs. Nesbit said.

Miranda stopped midchew and nodded. After she'd swallowed she said, "I love to eat."

"So I see," Mrs. Nesbit laughed. "Only soon you'd best start to watch it."

They were going from one unpleasant subject to another, and this fact alone caused Miranda to take larger bites than usual and move her eyes greedily over the food stacks. All this was interrupted by the jangling phone. Audrey Nesbit reached a

long arm over the table and plucked the wall receiver from its cradle.

"Olivia, what on earth are you calling about? The child is fine." She winked at Miranda and then listened. Her face froze and then switched to an expression of smug surprise. "In the country, darling?

But I thought, I mean, you *told* me you were in town working like a mole in its tunnel. Did I hear wrong? Where are you stuck? In what country?" She paused and lifted her eyebrows. "Vermont. Well, for heaven's sake. Two feet they've got. Surely someone can plow you out. I mean, certainly they are not unused to snow falling in quantity in the state of Vermont. Surely someone can get you out of there before Monday." Again she paused to listen, but this time she turned her back so Miranda could no longer watch the interesting play of feeling on her face. She did, however, see Mrs. Nesbit's shoulders slump. "I see, yes, well of course it can't be helped, as you say. Don't be silly, certainly she can stay the extra day. It doesn't put me out, much. She seems fine and really is no bother. I'll put her on." She passed the telephone to Miranda. "I suppose you know who it is."

"Hello, Randy." Olivia was talking fast. "Audrey says it's okay for you to stay the extra day and we really are snowbound, so just hang in there and we'll pick you up as soon as we can. Are there things to do? Are you bored?"

"I'm not bored," Miranda said.

"Good. We'll see you soon as we can."

Miranda hung up.

"So, you're here till Monday." Mrs. Nesbit shrugged. "Your mother is quite a lady." She looked unhappily at Miranda. "What are we going to do about you?"

"Don't trouble about me." Miranda got up quickly. "I really can be very occupied. I've just begun to study Dinah and her wardrobe."

Mrs. Nesbit looked confused. "Dinah?"

"That doll."

"Oh," Mrs. Nesbit sighed in great relief. "Listen, she's yours, my dear, lock, stock, and riding habit. You've got yourself a doll."

Miranda could not believe it. She clenched her hands on the back of the chair to keep from rushing up to Mrs. Nesbit and embracing her in a sloppy hug.

She had a beautiful doll. Plans were

forming in her mind. Other people had always made plans for her, but now she could scarcely believe all the secret, exciting plots that began to hatch in her head. Wouldn't they all be surprised if they knew, Miranda thought, as she mounted the steps to the attic. But they wouldn't know, for Miranda's first plan was that Dinah was her own secret.

4

On Tuesday Olivia and Alistair came for Miranda. Olivia made no pretense about having invented the story of work. Alistair hung back and didn't say a word. Audrey was not very pleasant nor was she about to tell Olivia that having Miranda for two extra days "had been a pleasure." She would only say that Miranda had not been a bother and had played by herself for three days, stopping only for eating and sleeping.

On the drive from Westport to the city, Alistair insisted on listening to continuous news while Olivia dozed. In the city dirty snow mounds flanked the curbs, and in a freezing wind Olivia and Miranda picked their way over the crusted piles toward their apartment building. Alistair slipped and slid behind them, carrying their luggage.

Miranda watched him nervously, for tucked into a soft sock in the satin compartment of her case was none other than the beautiful Dinah. Miranda carried the steamer trunk and the rest of Dinah's wardrobe in a shopping bag.

Up in her room Miranda unpacked the clothes in her suitcase. Then she closed her door as tightly as possible, given its warped edges, and quickly settled Dinah on the top shelf in the back of her enormous closet. Miranda had an unusual closet. It was one of the great things about living in an old building. The not-so-great things were the cracking plaster and leaking pipes. However, this closet was huge, deep enough to step into and sit down in and even keep a desk in. Behind the clothes rack and up its back wall were four shelves with clothes and papers on them. Miranda pushed

these aside and made room for Dinah's
steamer trunk. Then she shielded both the
doll and her trunk from view by piling
shoeboxes in front of them. Actually, there
was not much danger of anyone snooping
in Miranda's closet. Olivia was a great be-
liever in privacy. She made a point of

never rummaging through Miranda's things and she expected the same of Miranda. Miranda worked busily on her closet, for the plan that she had begun to develop had a great deal to do with that closet. It had always been a refuge for her. Now she had new plans that would make the closet more than just a refuge in which to hide and dream. It was to be a place in which things were going to happen.

5

"You've got no school again," Olivia wailed. She sat hunched over her breakfast coffee at the small kitchen table, huge round specs low on her narrow nose, glaring at her datebook. "Every other minute that place of learning you go to shuts down. What newfangled holiday have they cooked up this time?"

"Christmas." Miranda poured orange juice from a plastic pitcher into a small glass and sipped it while melting butter in an iron frying pan.

"Christmas? Don't tell me. Where is the time going this year? What'll you do? I forgot to sign you up with a vacation group.

What'll I do with you? Do you want to come to the office with me? Should I try to find somebody you can stay with?"

Miranda watched the butter begin to bubble and brown. She tapped an egg on the side of the pan and then opened it. "I never want to do that again," she said. "*Never.*"

Olivia blinked. "Really? Was it so terrible at Audrey's?"

"I'll be perfectly fine by myself," Miranda went on. "I have a million things to do."

"A million?" Olivia looked impressed. "Is this *my* Miranda? Won't you get bored when you're finished?"

Miranda flipped the egg expertly. "I said a million, Olivia, weren't you listening?"

"Excuse me, Randy, I have my lapses. Also I have a lecture to give to some dreary little group on Long Island. Who'll get your supper?"

"The same person who got my breakfast," Miranda said, sliding the egg onto a dish.

Again Olivia blinked and even looked a bit confused.

"Leave me some money for chopped chuck," Miranda went on.

"Miranda Perry, are you sure?" Olivia looked even more surprised.

Miranda nodded decisively. "By the way, what are you lecturing about?"

"Children's toys and how they encourage role playing. That subject always gets a lively question period afterward." Olivia looked at the kitchen clock. "Ouch, I didn't realize it was this late. I've got a whopping day. Editorial conference, department meeting, dinner with women's club, and lecture. I'd better get a move on." She took off her glasses, picked up the mug of black coffee, and took it with her into the bedroom. Now she was rushing, hurrying, too-busy-for-anything Olivia.

Miranda sipped her juice, salted her egg, and sat chewing slowly, waiting in a delicious state of anticipation for her mother to emerge and leave. Finally the door opened and a transformed Olivia appeared, red hair combed and shining, tall in brown suede pants and russet turtleneck, amber beads swinging to her belt, and buttery high-heeled boots, stepping quickly from sink to table to front hall closet, gathering her purse, briefcase, and

jacket. When everything was assembled she placed a kiss on top of Miranda's head.

"So long, Randy, have a lovely day. You're a peach to be so independent. If anything comes up and you need me, call the office. Linda will know where to find me. There's five dollars on top of the desk for food or whatever." She stuck her arms into the jacket sleeves and flung a long multicolored silk muffler round her neck.

"One last thing," Miranda said.

Olivia whipped around, hand on doorknob. "What?"

"Do you say anything about dolls?"

"Dolls? What are you talking about?"

"In the lecture tonight. Will you say anything about girls playing with dolls?"

"Miranda darling, are there any girls *left* who play with dolls?"

"Okay." Miranda nodded.

Olivia winked and swept out the door.

6

After she washed and dried the break-fast dishes and sponged crumbs off the table, Miranda with slow pleasure returned to her room. She had stood up to Olivia for Dinah's sake and it had worked. Hooray! She was actually unscheduled and on her own. Ungrouped, un-baby-sat. The day was hers. It was strange and wonderful that superorganized Olivia had forgotten to make a vacation plan for her and then had allowed her to be on her own. She put on a pair of soft, stretched-out jeans, a brown wool sweater, striped socks, and thick leather work shoes. Then she brushed her teeth, combed her hair, and cleaned her glasses. Finally she turned on the light in her closet, pushed the boxes and hanging clothes aside, and inspected the empty shelves. The bottom shelf was not empty. On it lay Dinah and her steamer trunk. Miranda selected a suitable daytime dress for the doll, a high-necked gray wool with white collar and small pearl buttons. She arranged the petticoat and the sash at the waist. She pulled a woolen coat of heather tweed trimmed with rabbit over the dress and placed a matching hat on Dinah's head. Then, carefully, she sat Dinah down in a tissue paper–lined shoebox she had prepared and put the box in a shopping bag. Miranda sat back on her heels to look at the effect of all this and she was pleased. She put on her pea jacket and earmuffs, got a spiral notebook and pen from her closet, took the key and the five-dollar bill off the desk, and with Dinah in tow left the apartment.

"It's a raw day," Pat the doorman noted as Miranda went past him. She tugged her mittens on with her teeth and kept walk-

ing, eyes straight, the shopping bag held rigidly at her side.

She had decided to do as much as possible by foot to avoid putting a dent in the five dollars. She walked several blocks down Madison Avenue and then turned east on Fifty-ninth Street. The day was raw and her nose lost feeling only slightly before the fingers of the hand that held the shopping bag. By the time she entered the tall building on Third Avenue, both hands were numb. She looked carefully at the exhibits of furniture and brilliant new wallpapers in the display windows in the lobby. When she had finished studying them, Miranda took a long look at the directory on the wall of the lobby. This building was filled with businesses that sold costly wallpapers, furniture, rugs, tiles, and bric-a-brac. She had passed it many times and had even ventured into the lobby before, but never to visit any offices. She selected the floors she needed and wrote them down in her spiral pad. Then she took the elevator up to the seventeenth floor. There were two or three wallpaper places up there.

Behind a thick glass door an unreal-looking, painted receptionist sat at a Lucite desk, a Lucite phone at her elbow and a white fur rug under her feet. Miranda opened the glass doors and approached the painted lady.

"Can I help you?" the lady inquired coolly.

"Not just yet, I'm looking," Miranda said back. It amazed her that this woman spoke at all. She resembled a plastic mannequin. She looked as if she had not only been painted, but varnished, too. Her mouth, nails, eyelids, cheeks, and hair had a high unnatural sheen. Miranda headed for the racks of wallpaper samples, which were hung on movable panels, and began to go through them, considering each one carefully.

"Is this for your bedroom, honey?" a loud voice said behind her.

"Not really," Miranda looked back at a very tall woman in an enormous fur hat, an even more enormous fur jacket, and out-size glasses.

"These are very expensive papers here," the woman went on. She was shuffling through from the opposite end of the rack. "Did your mommy tell you to come by?"

"No," said Miranda.

The woman laughed loudly. Everything about her was big. She had huge rings on her fingers and giant Indian bracelets stacked on either wrist.

"Well, you ought to tell your mother before you order, cookie, or she'll have herself a heart attack."

The cool mannequin at the Lucite desk giggled and uncrossed her shiny legs.

"Who told you to come up here?" she called.

"I looked in the Yellow Pages," Miranda replied. She didn't like all the questions.

"The Yellow Pages," the stiff at the desk repeated in shock. "We only cater to decorators. Didn't you read that part? We don't sell to people without a decorator."

The big woman nodded. "That's the truth, sweetheart. If you like one of these papers, you tell your mommy that a decorator has got to order it for you. I happen to be one and you can give her my card." She whipped a card case out of her of course enormous bag and presented a card to Miranda. "Mrs. Evie Small," it read.

Miranda looked at the last name and then back up at Mrs. Small, who burst out laughing. So did Miranda.

"Crazy, isn't it? I ought to change it, I guess, but people *do* remember me and what's wrong with a little joke?" She was pushing the panels around all the time she spoke. Miranda caught sight of one of the papers as it flew by and drew in her breath.

"That's the one," she said.

"Which?" Mrs. Small went back a few.

"That one. The one like velvet and silk."

"Mmmm." Mrs. Small studied it. "A beaut, kiddo, you've got good taste, but it's no child's room paper."

"I don't want child's room paper," Miranda snapped.

"Oh?" Mrs. Small looked curious. The receptionist strode over to listen. "What do you want it for?"

"I want it for a gallery."

"A gallery? What sort of gallery?"

"A room with a high ceiling, crystal chandelier, priceless paintings on the walls, and Oriental rugs. You know, a gallery," said Miranda impatiently. "Also, I could use some for a music room."

"Has anyone authorized you to manage this project?" Mrs. Small said.

"No one has to," said Miranda. "I thought it up and I shall do it myself."

The receptionist and Mrs. Small looked at each other.

"This paper has to be specially ordered,"

said the receptionist. "It's thirty dollars a roll."

"That's all right," Miranda said. "I can afford what I need."

"And, of course, you need to order through a decorator."

"I have one." Miranda read from the card, "A Mrs. Evie Small."

The receptionist held up her order form. "Name and address?" she said.

Miranda gave her the information.

"Okay, how much do you need?"

"I need ten inches by twelve," said Miranda.

Both women were speechless for a moment, then Mrs. Small narrowed her eyes and looked sharply at Miranda. "Wait a minute," she said. "Where is this gallery?"

"It's as you enter the house."

"Where is the house?"

"In the back of my closet." Miranda looked down. "It's a dollhouse I'm planning." She knelt down to take Dinah out of her shopping bag. "It's her house, actually."

Both women ogled Dinah.

"Why, she's beautiful," the receptionist said delightedly. She had become interested and friendly. "Me and my sister collect dolls and I know she's very, very special. Does she have a signature? Are there any initials on her?"

"Yes." Miranda pulled the collar of Dinah's coat and dress down at the back of her neck to reveal the letters H.R.G. impressed in the bisque. "She *is* very special and I want the best for her."

"You're right," said the receptionist.

Miranda was getting more talkative,

warmed by their interest, and she took her notebook out of the shopping bag. "You see, I'm going to make a beautiful place for her on these shelves I've got. Each shelf is a floor of her house." She showed them the rough drawing of the plan that she'd made. "This paper would be fine for her gallery. I'm going to partition the shelves and make alcoves and windows and collect beautiful things."

"How much money do you have to spend on this project?" said Mrs. Small.

"I have five dollars," said Miranda.

Mrs. Small looked very thoughtfully at the doll. "Listen, honey," she said. "You can have whatever scraps I've got left over. I have a foot of gorgeous carpet and I've got some samples of fantastic papers. Dusty," she turned to the receptionist, "you must have lots of swatches lying around."

The plastic-looking Dusty nodded. "I just love your doll." Her eyes were riveted on Dinah. "I mean, she's really fine. She's French bisque and no copy and those eyes are called paperweight glass because they're so deep."

"I know." Miranda forgot to be shy. "I just love her, too. I couldn't believe it when this lady gave her to me, just like that, and now I want to make her the most beautiful house in the world. A perfect house with everything exactly right. A music room and a sitting room and a gallery."

"And a conservatory," Mrs. Small put in. "Oh, make her a conservatory. It would be perfect for the period." .

"What is it?" said Miranda.

"A room full of potted palms and hanging ferns, all green and romantic. Dusty, you had a terrific ferny wallpaper. Give the kid a couple of inches, it should do the trick."

Dusty snapped her fingers, which wasn't easy with their endless polished orange nails, and went off on her spiked platforms.

"And then, kiddo, you come with me. I know some people you oughta meet."

Dusty came back with scraps of odd-sized paper. "Here," she said, sticking them into an envelope, "take these home and see if you can use them, and you really must meet my sister Mildred. She'll give you a call."

"Y'know who she oughta meet?" Mrs. Small said excitedly.

"Yes," Dusty said. "They'll go bananas when they see the doll."

"I have to pick something up over there now, so she can come with me."

"Where?" Miranda was breathless.

"The Grahams, sweety, they stock gorgeous antiques for the trade, but their passion is doll collecting. Wait a sec while I give Dusty my order and then we'll drop over there together."

Miranda hung back while Mrs. Small ordered some papers. She wondered if all this was really okay, was Mrs. Small on the level? Like any city kid, Miranda had been warned almost from birth *never* to take up with strangers, never to talk to them, and certainly not to accompany them anyplace.

What if Mrs. Small and Dusty simply wanted to get Dinah away from her and were cooking up a scheme to do it by talking to each other in some sort of code.

"Okay." Mrs. Small turned around, pulling the huge fur together with a clanking of bracelets. "We're off to see Jeremy Graham on Sixty-second Street."

"Oh, listen," Miranda said. "I can't, I mean, I just remembered my mom said I had to be home and I'm late."

"Suit yourself, honey," said Mrs. Small. "You've got my card if you need me."

Clutching her envelope of wallpapers and Dinah's bag, Miranda left the office.

"Oh say, listen," Dusty called after her. "If you want carpet samples try Tufson Carpets, room twelve fifty-seven. Tell Denise, Dusty sent you."

"Okay," Miranda called back. "Next time I'm around, and thanks very much."

She didn't go to Tufson because she thought she might meet Mrs. Small and be caught in a lie. At any rate, she had more to do than she could have imagined. She walked quickly up to her own neighborhood and began to get very hungry. The walk, the excitement, and the escape from a potentially evil plot by Mrs. Small had given her an appetite. The smells coming out of Sal's Pizza were enough to make her swoon. But she knew she had to check something before she spent a nickle of the five dollars. The something to check was at Bilk's Lumberyard.

"I need a sheet of heavy cardboard for walls," Miranda said, "and I want you to cut it according to my plan." She spread it on the desk in front of Bilk.

"What is it?" Bilk said. "A mouse run?"

"It's a dollhouse," Miranda said impatiently, "and those are arches and doors."

"Arches and doors I can't give you," said Bilk.

"You can't cut out an arch for me?" Miranda had never imagined this awful possibility. "I have a saw at home, but I couldn't, I mean, I can't get it straight." She was very upset. "I wanted everything to be perfect for Dinah."

"Dinah?" Bilk was only mildly interested.

"This is Dinah." Miranda took Dinah out of the shopping bag. "She's probably the most beautiful doll in the world. I can't give her sloppy arches and crooked doors."

Miranda was passionate on this point.

"Aw, look." Bilk was clearly not a "doll person," but he was certainly an "I-can't-stand-to-see-a-miserable-kid person." "Look, I'll run it through for you later, when I've got a break."

"For how much," said Miranda.

"Seven-fifty."

She hung her head and her voice was a whisper. "I can't go more than five."

"Five," Bilk barked. Then he repeated it, scratching his head and nodding. "Five. Now get outa here and don't send me your friends."

"When is your break?"

"Try me at three." He seemed very exasperated and Miranda knew it was time to vamoose.

As she passed Sal's Pizza she had a terrible moment. She ran the rest of the way home.

"Weather's warming up," said the doorman as she whizzed past him.

"You said it," Miranda called over her shoulder. "It's a beautiful day."

7

She worked feverishly all that day. The hours flew. She had a lunch of refrigerator remains and then proceeded to cut the wallpaper so all she'd have to do would be to paste it to the cardboard partitions. She went through magazines, selecting pictures suitable to hang as portraits in the gallery. Finally it was time to pick up the cardboard from Bilk's. After that her day was busier still. She stopped for a dinner of eggs, corn flakes, and ham and periodically stood up to stretch.

By nine o'clock she began to see the effect she was striving for. The closet shelves were transformed by partitions and papers

into a series of rooms that, even though empty, were cheerful and pleasant. Her plans were taking shape. As she worked, Miranda consulted a pile of library books that she had kept stacked on the floor of her closet. These were books about dolls and dollhouses as well as about famous doll collections. From them she had learned that Dinah was French and that she was a collector's doll, initialed by her famous

French maker on the back of her neck. She was in excellent condition and her vast wardrobe made her even more valuable. The settings in the book illustrations were perfect for Dinah. The rooms as well as the dolls themselves were in a world as far from the one Olivia and Miranda knew as a distant planet. It was a world of order and gaiety, of mothers and fathers and cousins and aunts and uncles and family outings and holiday festivities, of hugs and pony-rides and mulled wine around the fireplace. It was the world that Miranda longed to inhabit, a world in which no one said, "If anything comes up, call Linda, she'll know where to find me," or "Would you like to come to the office," or "Should I find someone you can stay with." Miranda sat looking at the picture books and dreaming of her lovely world until she was jolted by the sound of Olivia's key in the lock and Olivia herself in the foyer calling.

"Randy, you up? God, it's bloody cold out there. Where are you?"

"In my room. I'll be right in." Quickly

she pushed the books out of sight and swept the last bits of wallpaper over the sill and shut the closet door.

Olivia appeared in her room. Her nose and chin were red and she looked very tired. "Come in and have some tea with me. I am the original frozen turnip."

"Okay," Miranda followed her into the kitchen.

"They give you awful meals at these meetings. Ten-year-old buzzard and mealy peas, yech. What did you do today to keep yourself from getting bored."

Miranda cupped her chin in her palm. She gave Olivia her owl look. "Was everybody there a sociologist?"

"No, this was a women's club."

"Did they agree with all your points of view?"

"It's hard to tell, but the important thing is that I like to feel I've started them thinking, shaken them up a bit, given them a new idea or two." Olivia put tea in a pot and poured boiling water over it.

"Did you talk about dolls?"

"Not exactly. I told them about you, though, and how you had no interest whatsoever in your dolls, but loved your trucks. What if I had forced you to play with dolls, pressured you to play with them because you are a girl? What if I had never bought you trucks and model planes at all?" Olivia poured the tea into mugs, her face intent and serious. "Even though those were the toys you liked."

"What were your toys?" said Miranda.

"My toys?" Olivia frowned. She blew into her mug. "I hated them. I had dumb doll after dumb doll with a couple of nurse's kits in between. No one ever dreamed of giving me a truck. Those all went to my brother Roger. What I really wanted were my brother's toys, my brother's freedom, my brother's life. I had to plead with him to allow me to touch one of his model planes. My parents would never get me toys like Roger's. They let me know how odd it was of me to even want them. I spent my time pretending to be a person I wasn't, trying to be like everybody else. I was supposed to be a good little girl and play with dumb little dolls and do what everyone expected of me, while Roger was going to grow up and have an exciting job and do what he liked. That's why I've wanted so much to give you freedom, Miranda. I don't want you to have to struggle for your freedom the way I did."

"What was the struggle?" said Miranda.

"Oh." Suddenly Olivia looked distracted and tired. She yawned.

Miranda knew the signs. The conversation was over. Olivia's mind was on something else.

"Wow, I guess I'm bushed. We'll save Olivia's struggles for another time."

Her mother's past, Miranda thought, was locked up in a box labeled NOT TO BE DISCUSSED. Olivia took a sip of tea, got up, stretched, and declared she was ready for bed.

8

Piecing together Olivia's mysterious past from words dropped here and there was a pet hobby of Miranda's. It wasn't that Olivia had planned to keep her past a secret, just that if it were all known it would embarrass her. Olivia wanted to forget it as much as possible. The fact was that Miranda's father was neither the butcher nor the actor, as some people said. Olivia had married him as she had played with her dolls, to be like everyone else in the town where she had grown up. They had married one week after graduating from college. Olivia had worn a white wedding gown and he had placed a diamond-studded circle of gold on her finger. They had cut a tiered wedding cake and two hundred guests had applauded.

Eleven months later Miranda was born and eleven months and three weeks after that Olivia decided that she was finished with trying to be like everyone else. She wanted to go back to school. Her husband thought she should stay home and take care of her baby. She wanted a career. Her husband objected. They quarreled and disagreed about everything. Olivia packed her bags and her baby and with the help of her loving but confused parents traveled to New York, where she moved in with an old college friend and found both a sitter for Miranda and a lawyer for her divorce.

One sunny morning soon after she arrived in New York something happened to Olivia that changed her life in the months and years to come. She set out to find a job. Determined not to be a burden to her parents or to the husband she had left, she had decided to work on a master's degree at night and work to support herself and

Miranda during the day. In college Olivia had taken a course in computer technology and had done very well. An agency sent her to an office high over Park Avenue where she was interviewed and then tested.

She liked the office. The pay was good and the hours perfect to fit around her courses. There were several applicants for the job, but only Olivia and a young man were asked to stay. The interviewer called Olivia back into his office. He was a mild-mannered pudgy man. He gazed at her sweetly from his side of the desk and then, smiling, opened his palms helplessly. "I don't know what to say," he began. "You really scored very high on the test, higher than anybody else, and I like you, but . . ." he paused.

Olivia waited, confused, wondering what had gone wrong.

"To put it bluntly, I think this way," he continued. "I've got this guy here who has a wife and kid to support and I look at you and I think, a lovely dish like that is surely being taken care of by her husband or she will be soon enough, and even though this guy didn't score that high, to be honest with you, he really *needs* the job. You see, it just isn't right not to give it to him."

Olivia's throat went dry. She could hardly speak. "Listen," she blurted, "I need the job. I'm divorced. I have a kid. I . . ."

"Sure, sure. But soon you'll meet another guy and he'll have you up to here in furs and diamonds." He touched his forehead. "Believe me, you're that kind of dish."

For one of the few times in her life Olivia was speechless. She stood up and ran out of the office. She knew there was nothing she could have said to change the man's mind.

Later Olivia did find a job, but her experience on that bright day fired her with the energy and anger that resulted in her master's thesis in sociology. The thesis was an impassioned work full of the new and provocative ideas about women that were beginning to be expressed at that time. When the thesis was published it caused a stir. Olivia was soon lecturing and editing. She began teaching a course and writing a column as well as working on a new magazine. She appeared on television, reviewed books, and wrote articles. She helped found a bookshop called New Woman, which featured reading material that answered the needs of the "new woman." It carried some children's books and not one of them concerned a doll, with the exception of a book in which the doll was owned by a little boy.

Olivia's refusal to discuss her childhood with anyone gave rise to all kinds of outrageous rumors. She did nothing to stop them, for she enjoyed them. The truth would have been more embarrassing than any sensational story. Miranda's father had remarried, sold insurance, and had a large family in their hometown. Olivia's parents were dead, and her brother Roger was a dentist in San Francisco. Her old life had been a painful trap, and as far as she was concerned she had not been truly born until the day she arrived in New York.

But Miranda loved the idea of Olivia's childhood and was even envious of it. How could Olivia have hated two cozy parents who pressed food, gifts, and dolls on her. Miranda's images of Olivia's childhood were tinged with a golden light. She couldn't understand why they aroused such dark and complicated feelings in her mother.

Miranda went back to her room, thinking about all these curious things and the secrets she kept about her mother's past. She'd never divulged any of it to a soul. Someone like Audrey Nesbit would love to get her hands on the information.

What and who was Olivia to Miranda? Olivia was her mother. Strong and energetic and full of opinions. She was a super planner, but she could mow Miranda down. She was enthusiastic, but she didn't always listen to Miranda. She was very, very busy. She was still, Miranda supposed,

trying to prove she was as good as Roger.
"If something happened and I really
needed her, she'd drop everything," Miranda said out loud. She undressed slowly.
She folded her jeans and arranged her
sweater over the back of a chair. Slowly she
put on a pair of old pajamas. Before getting into bed, she walked into her closet to
take a last admiring look at the miracles
she was creating on the back shelves. She

took off Dinah's day dress and put on her frilled cotton nightgown and lay her down in the shoebox.

"Something else, Dinah, my dear," she whispered to the doll. "Olivia's original name happened to be Mary Lou."

9

When Miranda came into the kitchen the next morning, Olivia was talking rapidly into the telephone that was tucked under her chin while she mixed up some orange juice. "Okay," she was saying, "it sounds fine over here. I'll tell her. So long, then." She put the juice down and hung up the phone. "Hey, Miranda," she said brightly. Miranda was immediately on her guard. She knew that bright tone always meant danger.

"I was just talking to Alistair and he says Towny's on vacation, too, only she's going bats with boredom. She'd just love to come by and spend the day with you, and I thought since you're such a resourceful person . . ."

"She's coming here?" Miranda couldn't believe it would be that bad. "Today?"

"Oh dear," Olivia moaned. "I did something wrong, but Randy, you know how you've wanted a friend, and she'd really love to come, and you haven't anything planned, have you?"

"You didn't ask me first," Miranda said.

"I know, you're right." Olivia looked totally crestfallen. "That was an awful thing for me to have done."

They were both silent, thinking. Miranda was thinking that this was Olivia at her worst, pushing her around, setting things up for her without even asking so that *her* life was easier. Now she was stuck. If she made too big a stink about this date Olivia might become suspicious about how she was spending her time.

Olivia was thinking that she must stop pushing Miranda around and setting things up for her without asking.

"I'll call Alistair back and tell him it's off," Olivia said.

"No," Miranda said dully. "It's okay."

"Thank you, Randy, I'll never do this to you again." Olivia kissed her and sighed with relief. "Maybe you'll even enjoy it."

Towny arrived at eleven o'clock, putting a complete halt to all Miranda's lovely plans with Dinah.

"Hi ya." She threw her pea jacket on the hall bench, shook out her ponytail, looked around the dim hall, and forged into the living room. "Got any records?" She folded into a deep canvas chair, knees apart, and started flipping through Olivia's meager collection of discs. She made disappointed noises through her teeth.

Miranda sat down awkwardly on the sofa opposite and with a sinking heart watched her guest. She was thinking when, oh when, would Towny go home? And what, oh what, would she do with her until that blessed moment?

What they did on that endless day was the following. First Towny read some magazines. Then they watched television soap operas, then went down to Sal's for pizza (Alistair's treat). Then they came back and watched more television. At three o'clock, during a commercial, Towny rolled over on the floor and asked if she could see Olivia's clothes. "I really dig rags. I want to be a model. Alistair says I've got flair."

"I don't go in Olivia's closet," Miranda said.

"You don't?" Towny was amazed. "I'm always in my mother's things. Drawers, closets, make-up, everything. It's great. She leaves everything all over the place. I read her love letters."

"To Alistair?"

"You've got to be kidding." Towny stood up. "She ditched old Al officially five years ago, but before that they had what I guess you'd call an open marriage. My mother has always had some jerk on the string. C'mon, let's have a look at Olivia's stuff."

"No," said Miranda, "we can't do that. She doesn't do it to me and I don't do it to her."

Towny sat down again, frowning and sullen. "Big deal. Big secret stuff. Boy, you should see what I get out of my mom's drawers. Everything you ever wanted to know about sex but were afraid to ask."

Miranda panicked. She sensed that Towny now wanted to get into *that* subject.

"Does your mother tell you much?" was Towny's next question.

Miranda was right.

"She tells me everything," said Miranda miserably, "and I don't want to hear it."

"You're some nut" was Towny's verdict.

It was true. This was yet another aspect of Miranda's poor show at being Olivia's daughter. Olivia *did* want to explain sex to her, with every book, diagram, and colored chart prepared on the subject. But Miranda didn't want to hear it. Not one word. And now here was Towny with that look in her eyes that meant she was throbbing to get on with the subject.

"Look," Miranda said, trying desperately to think of something to divert Towny, "how are you going to get into modeling? I mean, have you got a plan?"

"Uh-huh, I've got a few plans up my sleeve. I've also got a couple of top-priority bits of info that I think your mother would love to know about. I'll pass them on to you, Miranda, if we go have a look at the clothes and stuff."

"No," Miranda said flatly. "I said no before and I say no again. No no no no no."

"Okay okay okay okay." Towny looked threateningly. "But I wasn't kidding. I *do* know a few things your mother doesn't. You two are headed for hard times, kid."

"What are you talking about?" Miranda's voice shook. Towny had succeeded in frightening her.

"Mum's the word. A secret for a secret."

"I don't believe you."

"Up to you, but you'll find out soon enough, and you'll be sorry you didn't know sooner."

"You couldn't know anything about Olivia."

"Couldn't I? Alistair's head of her department. I pick things up, as you know. My ears flap in the breeze." She paused for all this to take effect. "Let's have a look in Olivia's room."

Miranda shook her head vehemently.

"Suit yourself."

They watched the three-o'clock movie without saying another word to each other. At five Towny got up, stretched, put on her jacket, and walked out of the room. Miranda followed her to the front door and waited there until the elevator came. As the elevator door was about to close Towny called out, "So long, jerko."

Miranda said "So long" to the empty hall. Then she went back to her room, fell onto her bed, and burst into what became a long luxurious bout of sobbing. She was mostly furious to have given up a precious day to the awful Towny. Also, she was scared by some of the things Towny had said. Miranda wondered what Towny knew about Olivia? What was her information? Was there something going on that could hurt Olivia? Miranda was very unsettled. She knew that in a way Alistair was Olivia's boss, and therefore Towny could have picked up information. Miranda stood up and went to her closet and turned on the light and moved aside the boxes. There was the small world she'd begun to create for Dinah. Unfinished as it was, the papered rooms gave off a glow of peace that was comforting. Soon Miranda was searching among her growing collection of boxes and papers and magazines for scraps that could work in Dinah's house. A pocket mirror for the gallery, an old watch box for a living room chest. Before long she had forgotten all about Towny.

At seven Olivia came home. "How'd it go with Townsend?" She waited to ask the question until they were preparing dinner in the kitchen.

"Terrible," said Miranda.

"Oh, Randy, is she that bad? She seemed so nice that time we met. So outgoing and spunky."

"Her idea of an afternoon's fun was going through your closet and drawers."

"Oh dear," Olivia wailed. "Did you?"

"Of course not." Miranda was shocked. "Do you think I'd let her do a thing like that?"

Olivia turned from the pot she'd been stirring to look at Miranda. It was a long

75

and searching look, unusual for Olivia. "Miranda, you really are full of surprises. I know sometimes I bother you and your stubborn streak can drive me up the wall. You can be so damned uncooperative. I'm not always easy to be with myself, but this week you've been really fantastic. You've been responsible, capable, self-reliant . . ." she paused to think for a moment ". . . aside from which you're a good person. I'm glad that you're my kid and you stood up to Towny. I'm sure it wasn't easy."

"Yeah." Miranda was embarrassed by all the praise. "She called me a jerk and didn't tell me some big-deal secret information she had."

"About what?"

"You."

Olivia looked alarmed. She stopped stirring for a moment and her face was tired, even haggard. Then she pushed some hair off her forehead, took a deep breath, and began to stir again. "Well, let's not concern ourselves with Towny's fantasies," she said.

But Miranda had seen enough to suspect

that they were not fantasies and that Olivia was very, very concerned. So concerned and preoccupied that superorganized Olivia had forgotten to sign her into a vacation group for this Christmas and New Year break.

10

When the phone woke her the next morning, Miranda was in the middle of a dream in which Towny had gotten locked in her closet while snooping and they couldn't get her out. Groggily she ran toward the kitchen. It was late. Olivia had gone already, and a note was tacked to the bulletin board: "See you at six."

"Hello?" Miranda said.

"Hello," It was a young voice and an unsure one. "You don't know me. I'm Dusty Munson's sister Mildred. Dusty told me about your doll and I wondered if I could see her. I ummmm," she lowered her voice, "I love dolls." Miranda didn't answer because she was still half asleep. The voice went on nervously. "Maybe you don't remember Dusty?"

"I do, I do." Miranda woke up a notch. "She has long nails."

"The longest," said Mildred. "Well, anyway, she told me about your doll and I'm dying to see her and maybe you'd like to see mine and my dollhouse, which is pretty sensational."

"Where do you live?" said Miranda. A sudden rush of excitement and adventure made her now very wide awake. She was actually arranging a date, not through Olivia but completely by herself, without Olivia's even knowing about it. Mildred gave her the address, which was only blocks away, and Miranda said she'd be over as soon as she got dressed and ate breakfast.

Quickly she got into her clothes, all the while chewing a heel of bread. She put Dinah in a plaid dress and matching shawl and arranged her in the shopping bag. Suddenly Miranda's thoughts were in a state of confusion. Why was she going, she wondered? Who was this Mildred? What kind of house would it be? What was she getting into? She sat down on her bed. What had seemed so simple on the telephone now seemed very complicated. Should she go? Was this a mistake? Her head began to throb. "We'll just walk over and take a look at the building," she told Dinah. She put on her jacket and, with Dinah in the shopping bag, left the apartment.

She walked quickly because it was cold and because she wanted to get it over with and go home. When she got to the building she was surprised to see that it was one of the snappy-looking new ones in striped yellow and white brick with terraces, air conditioning, and a uniformed doorman blowing on white-gloved hands.

"Can I help you, miss?" he asked.

Miranda felt trapped. She had dawdled a moment too long in the entryway.

"Who do you wish to see?" He eyed her suspiciously.

"Mildred Munson," said Miranda, only

to prove that she was not just hanging around and hoping he would be embarrassed.

"Oh, Millie, is it?" He poked a button on the intercom. "What's your name?"

"I'm Miranda."

"Miranda's coming up," he called into the hole in the wall, "Take the first elevator on the right up to twenty-three, it's apartment K," he shouted after Miranda.

There was no escaping now. She found herself in a metallic-papered elevator rising with a hum to a very high floor. The door opened onto a long carpeted corridor painted green and punctuated by black doors with peepholes centered in them. At the very end of the corridor one of these doors stood open and in the doorway stood a curious-looking gnomelike girl. She was skinny and sallow, and the green hall light cast a greenish tinge on her narrow cheeks. Her eyes were huge and serious, her hair long and straight, and she wore a funny sacklike brown dress and red stockings.

She put out a hand as Miranda approached. "I'm Millie," she said. "I thought you'd probably change your mind and not come."

"I *said* I'd come," Miranda answered hastily. She was afraid for a moment that Millie was going to cry, but when they stepped into the brightly lit foyer she realized it was just Millie's odd expression. Her thin down-turned features in repose gave the impression of misery. Millie took Miranda's jacket and placed Dinah in her shopping bag reverently on a bench.

"My sister said Dinah is a real collector's doll. I have some copies from that period, but no originals." She led Miranda through a large low-ceilinged living room into a small tidy bedroom, explaining, "I share this with Dusty. My folks work, Dusty works, and I'm on vacation."

"I'm on vacation, too," said Miranda.

"Lucky us."

Miranda thought she was being sarcastic, but when she saw Mildred's forlorn grin, she knew the remark was meant seriously. Mildred was *very* serious. Her room looked

like something out of a ladies' magazine ar-
ticle: "How to Decorate a Small Room for
Two Girls Making the Most of Color and
Space." There were plastic cubes for books

and records, matching curtains and bedspreads covered with yellow and white daisies, and two yellow drop-leaf desks. But the most striking object in the room stood on its own platform in the corner. It was a three-story dollhouse, of intricate and elaborate design, stuffed with furniture, miniatures of all sorts, and dolls.

"Come meet the family," Mildred said. She knelt before the house and lined up the array of dolls, about ten in all, who dwelt there. She introduced them each by name: the Gilberts, Ned and Sarah, Mallory the butler, and Edith the guest. She made them each take a small bow. After the last introduction she said, "And now will you present Dinah?"

Miranda lifted Dinah out of the shopping bag. Millie drew in her breath. "Oh, she is a dream."

Inspired by Millie's awed interest, Miranda told her the entire story of Dinah, how she had been found at Mrs. Nesbit's and all the work she had done on her house. She told her the games she had in-

vented and the fact that Dinah was a secret
from Olivia. This last piece of information
interested Mildred the most.

"I don't tell anybody at school about my dolls," she said. "They might tease because I suppose I'm too old to play with them. But I'd never keep them a secret at home. Dusty and my parents love the dollhouse. My father built it and Dusty and Mom helped me furnish it." Mildred's parents owned a hardware store and her dollhouse was full of ingenious hinged and knobbed cupboards, drawers, and doors. "This house was Daddy's passion," she said. "When he finished it, he said he wished he was small enough to move in."

They marched Dinah through the rooms.

"Sit here, my dear, it's very comfy," Mildred advised, and down sat Dinah on a love seat to be joined by the Gilberts. Soon they invited Dinah for dinner. They all went below to the kitchen, where the cupboards were opened and their contents of pots, pans, table silver, and serving dishes exhibited. Before long a flurry of preparation was under way, the table in the dining room set, Teresa the baby doll being sent up for a nap and throwing a tantrum, Mallory in a dither. When the dolls finally sat down to dinner, Mildred paused and said she was very hungry herself. It was three o'clock in the afternoon.

In the Munsons' immaculate kitchen Millie turned up a pot of cold stew and a loaf of bread. They heated the stew and warmed the bread. When they finished eating and talking about school (Mildred, it seemed, was about as popular as Miranda), the winter sky was turning dark.

"I've got to go," Miranda said. "I hope you can come over." She dusted the crumbs off her lap and looked at the floor. "Because I really had a good time."

"Me, too," Millie nodded. They packed Dinah up, Millie gave Miranda her phone number and they said good-bye.

Walking home in a biting winter wind, Miranda felt light and warm. A friend. She had made a friend on her own, without help or assistance. She looked into the shopping bag at Dinah. She had to admit there had been help after all.

11

"**W**e are going to have a party to welcome in the New Year," Olivia said on the fourth morning of Miranda's vacation. "Some friends for supper and champagne."

That was how it began, innocently and casually. On her free evenings Olivia flipped through her collection of cookbooks, discussed this or that dish, and made lists.

"Who's coming?" Miranda finally asked.

"Just a few people from the magazine and the department of sociology."

"Alistair?"

"Un-huh." Olivia looked up from *The*

New York Times Cook Book. "Yes, Alistair and — Miranda, don't fly off the handle, but I couldn't get out of it."

"Townsend's coming too," Miranda finished the sentence.

"Yes, she's with him for the holidays. I couldn't tell him to leave her alone on that special night."

"I know," said Miranda. She'd known all along.

The party began to take shape. Olivia ordered loads of food. There would be ham and goose and pumpkin bread and sweet potato casserole and pâté. The party preparations rumbled outside Miranda's door all through the remaining days of her vacation. For Miranda those days were filled with Dinah's house, visits from Mildred, working on the rooms and furnishings, and trips to Dusty's office. Dusty had sent them to Tufson Carpets, where they had asked for Denise and been given some beautiful carpet and tile samples. Dusty also sent them to a fabric showroom on the same floor and they'd been handed a fat envelope full of pieces of silk and brocade and velvet. With the fabric, glue, scissors, and a collection of boxes, Mildred had shown Miranda how to make a banquette for the gallery, two window seats, and a bed. When they weren't actually working on the house they were moving Dinah and the other dolls through one of the many dramas they loved. The days passed in the loveliest ways. It was a relief to be on her own. It was a relief to have a friend.

On Christmas eve Miranda and Olivia were invited to dinner at the apartment of Olivia's first roommate in New York. There were ten old friends who exchanged gifts and reminiscences of their early days in the city. Miranda received two books, a painted box from India, a glass object called a "passion meter" which made the purple liquid inside bubble when you held it in a warm hand (if you were passionate), a muffler, a pair of mittens and a flowering cactus in a tiny pot (just right for the conservatory).

The next morning, Christmas day, Olivia

gave Miranda a turquoise ring. Miranda gave Olivia a pair of fleece-lined gloves she had saved up for and kept hidden since Thanksgiving. After exchanging presents, Miranda watched television and then worked on Dinah's house while Olivia re-wrote an article.

At first Miranda paid no attention to Olivia's party. Olivia took parties seriously. She planned every step. And although she was distracted and, Miranda thought, unu-sually preoccupied, she had fastened on the party with as much enthusiasm as ever. This party seemed her most serious.

Before long the parcels of food were being delivered, and Olivia in blue jeans and oversize apron was stirring and baking and chopping and tasting. On the day of the party the large living room was com-pletely overhauled, vacuumed, oiled, and waxed. Then the long table was heaped with arrangements of china, silver, nap-kins, and bowls of flowers. By nine o'clock in the evening crackers and pâté were ar-ranged in rows on platters under plastic wrap, champagne was cooling in the refrigerator, and everything else was warming in the oven. Olivia in black velvet pants and silver tunic basted the goose and consulted her watch.

"Are you going to change, Miranda? They'll be here any minute."

"All right." Miranda, out of sorts and full of doubts about the evening, went to her room. Without looking in the mirror, she pulled on the long skirt and matching blouse Olivia had tactfully left on her bed. The skirt was an elastic-waisted green with an orange band at the hem, which made Miranda look like a potted Christmas tree. To complete this look, Miranda placed an orange bow on top of her head. As she did, the doorbell rang. It was a lady who had driven down from Croton.

"Driving is dreadful," Miranda heard her say. "I skidded and slid all the way. Olivia, Happy New Year, my dear. Ah, hallo, Miranda, remember me, Lydia Fenwick?"

Miranda didn't, but nodded and shook

her hand, and the doorbell rang again.
These were people from the magazine,
four of them. They had shared a taxi and
probably, Miranda thought, a couple of
drinks, for they seemed unusually merry.
Four more people arrived. They worked at
the university and seemed even merrier.
Miranda knew everyone was supposed to
be brainy, and soon arguments, jests,

quips, and puns sailed around the room at a rate that made her head spin as she moved about with the tray of crackers and pâté.

"Oh thanks, pet," or "Yes, lovely," were the comments that were thrust her way.

"Where's Alistair?" Lydia Fenwick said.

"He should be here soon," Olivia said uncertainly.

"Is he bringing the nymphet?" This from a very tall man.

"The what?" said a woman.

"That delicious child. You know he's got a beauty there."

"Yes, he's bringing her." Olivia's eyes sought out Miranda's, but Miranda held the blankest of her looks.

"She is something, my friends," the lady named Fenwick said. "But, Howard, don't make her into a beastly little sex object, she's far too good for that. Great style and dash and clever, too."

The doorbell rang. Miranda didn't have to turn around to see who was there. The next thing she heard above the din was:

"Hi there, I'm Townsend, Alistair's brat."
When Miranda did turn around she bore
the tray of pâté in front of her like a shield.
"Oh, hi, Miranda." Towny seemed neu-
tral. She also seemed taller and even thin-
ner in a long skirt of denim patches. She

looked more than ever like a young Olivia. She took a cracker. "Thanks. My, isn't *somebody* a busy, busy girl." She loaded the cracker with pâté in maddeningly small amounts and then turned around as if Miranda had become a piece of furniture. As she headed back to the kitchen for a refill of crackers, Miranda heard Towny strike up a conversation with the tall man.

Olivia came into the kitchen. "Now don't let her get to you, Randy. I really don't think she knows what she's about. She thinks she's charming."

"So does everybody else," said Miranda. "She's not so dumb."

"Come on, Miranda," Olivia whispered impatiently. Miranda knew what she meant was "Don't bug me with your problems or go blank and sullen and lumpish and *ruin my party!*" Of course, all these unspoken messages were just enough to make Miranda go Blank, Sullen, and Lumpish. She was convinced that if Olivia had the chance to select a daughter that very moment

Towny would have been chosen, hands down.

Miranda arranged a new circle of crackers on the platter and trudged back into the living room. The party was now in what she supposed you'd call "full swing." Everybody was talking, laughing, drinking, and smoking. Towny stood between her father and the tall man, twirling a glass of something between her fingers until some of it splashed out and down the front of her blouse.

"Oooooops. Oh, that feels lovely," she smiled delightedly. "Where's your john, Miranda? I've got to wring out my little chest."

Miranda pointed sullenly down the long hall. "First door on the left." As Towny took off, she overheard the tall man say, "Alistair, how did you do it, old man. You've raised a splendid girl there."

By now Miranda had become a rotating fixture, rather like a lazy Susan. She picked up trays and passed them around and re-

filled them when they were bare. She returned empty glasses to the bar at the desk
and even poured out drinks. Olivia had
taught her to do all this years before and
she did it very well. In fact, one of her
greatest compliments had come in the middle of a party such as this when someone

suggested to Olivia that she rent Miranda out to a catering service. Big deal.

Olivia called her into the kitchen. Quickly they filled the champagne glasses on the trays. Miranda took one tray and Olivia the other.

As they returned to the living room Alistair was saying, "Hey, listen to the bells. It's Happy New Year everyone."

Champagne was passed around, everybody was kissing each other or tapping glasses together and saying Happy New Year. There was the sound of a cranking noisemaker from the street below. Olivia and Miranda went back to the kitchen to bring in the supper. For a while Miranda was very busy bringing in hot platters and serving dishes, so she didn't notice that Towny had been out of the room for a long time. She only realized this when she saw Towny enter the living room after all the others had helped themselves to food and were sitting and eating. Towny walked up to the buffet, took a dish, and heaped it with food. She glanced at Miranda, and her face was flushed with an odd merry look. "Happy New Year," she said.

Miranda was filled with foreboding.

12

"**H**ow delicious," the big man said. "Olivia, you've outdone yourself."

Everyone agreed.

"Did you make a contribution to this feast, Miranda?" said a small kindly looking woman. "Have you inherited Olivia's culinary gifts?"

"Come now, Jill," Lydia Fenwick laughed, "culinary gifts are as uninheritable as they are sexually determined. Don't force Miranda into any kitchens, please."

"Heavens, no." Jill pretended to be shocked. "I would never impose a sexist stereotype in this house. After all, we all know that Miranda Perry is the young indi-

vidualist who gave her dolls away at the
tender age of six."

"After having been bored to tears by
them," Olivia added proudly.

"I forgot that part, I haven't read your
essays for a few years."

Towny let out a whoop followed by what
seemed to be a seizure. Everyone stopped
what they were doing and saying. She was
choking on a piece of food or laughing or
both. Her cheeks were red and her eyes

watering and awful noises came out of her. Alistair leaped up and pounded on her back. She gasped and drew in a breath and then began to laugh.

"Townsend, what are you doing?" said Alistair.

"Threw away her dolls at six?" Towny gasped. "You should see what goes on in her room."

"Her room?" Olivia looked confused.

"It's not my *room*," Miranda cried.

"All right then, your closet. She's got a whole entire *dollhouse* in her closet. Doll this and doll that, doll clothes and doll furniture and doll books. It's all stuck in the back with boxes in front to hide it. She's a *doll freak*." This cracked Towny up so that once again she couldn't speak.

At first Miranda felt nothing. She put her head down and felt a burning sensation from neck to brow. Everyone in the room was still. No one, it seemed, even chewed. The room had become heavy with embarrassment.

Olivia cleared her throat. "Well, my

goodness," she said shakily. "As you can see, Miranda and I lead very private lives. We don't meddle or spy or interfere with each other."

Miranda knew from her voice that Olivia was horribly hurt. She had never heard that tone before.

"Townsend, you naughty girl," Alistair chided. "Did you snoop in Miranda's closet?" He tried for a light tone, but it didn't work.

Towny grew gloomy. Her moment was over and it hadn't turned out to be the big joke she'd planned. Nobody laughed. Everyone simply looked mortified.

The small woman named Jill who'd started the whole thing seemed determined to save the situation. "Well then," she said, smiling hopefully, "I would love to see your dolls, Miranda dear. I adored playing with dolls as a little girl. I had a collection of foreign dolls all in native costume. You know, I still like to take them out from time to time to give them an airing."

"It isn't dolls," Miranda said. "It's just one."

"May I see her, too?" Olivia said with what Miranda knew was a phony flourish of enthusiasm. "Maybe I'll get to know my daughter."

There wasn't any way out of it. Miranda got up. Jill, Olivia, Lydia Fenwick, and Towny followed her back to her bedroom. Towny had left the door to the closet open but had shoved the screen of boxes back into place. Miranda turned on the closet light and removed the boxes. Dinah sat on a divan made of a box covered with silk cut-velvet. She was wearing the faded calico Miranda had found her in and she looked just as cool and serene as ever.

"Why, Miranda." Olivia's mouth fell open. "You've done all this?"

"Not her clothes. She came with those. Audrey Nesbit gave me the clothes along with Dinah. We've done her house, though."

"*We?*"

"Me and my friend Mildred."

"Your friend Mildred?" Olivia sounded like a parrot.

"What a lot you've done," said Lydia Fenwick.

Miranda nodded. "I've spent hours and hours on it."

"Not only is it lovely, my dear, but let me tell you that doll and her wardrobe are worth a small fortune. Remember that when you've outgrown her and are short of money. You can cash her in for a bundle. Better than insurance or a savings account, for she's fun to play with in the meantime." Lydia Fenwick winked.

Miranda turned off the light and closed the door. There was no need to stack up the screen of boxes.

Silently they went back into the living room. Alistair was getting into his coat. "Towny, the hour is late and it's time we headed home."

Then everyone was at the door putting on coats and mufflers and saying good-bye and Happy New Year and Many More, and soon the room was empty. Miranda and Olivia turned to face the soiled dishes, glasses, and heaped ashtrays. Without speaking they changed out of their party clothes and systematically began to stack, scrape, and clean up. Olivia filled the sink with soapy water while Miranda brought in the dishes. Olivia's brow was deeply furrowed. She was lost in thought. "Thank you for your help tonight, Randy," she said. "There's a lot I have to talk to you about, but it's too late now. I guess it can wait. It's waited this long already."

"I'm sorry," said Miranda.

"For what?" said Olivia.

Miranda really couldn't say for what. For being Miranda, was all she could think of.

13

They didn't get to talk the next day because Olivia received a telephone call early in the morning and had to leave for an urgent meeting. Miranda went over the events of the party as she rearranged the boxes and furniture at the back of her closet. She also allowed herself to enjoy several daydreams in which Towny was humiliated and shamed and in which she, Miranda, was the heroine. All these thoughts kept Miranda from the big awful one of the "talk" she was going to have with her mother. It was in the middle of an especially lovely fantasy, in which Towny stupidly blabbed a piece of gossip concerning her father, that Miranda was interrupted by the telephone ringing.

"Is your mother at home?" said an unpleasant voice.

"No. Can I take a message?"

"When do you expect her?"

"This evening." Miranda used her most efficient tone. "Who shall I say called?"

"This is Rosamond Kessler from the university and you can tell her that I'm really awfully surprised to find that her things are still in the desk which is now *my* desk since we've switched offices. It was my understanding that her things were to be out of here by the first of the year and that is today."

"Should I write that down?" Miranda was no longer efficient, just confused. The woman sounded threatening.

"You can remember the gist of it, I'm sure. I'll tell her the rest." The woman hung up.

Miranda couldn't go back to her daydreams, she was too preoccupied by Rosamond Kessler's call. What right had that woman to push Olivia around? Miranda was amazed that anybody could talk that way to Olivia, even if it was through a messenger. Miranda did a little work on the dollhouse, creating the illusion of a window by placing a piece of blue colored paper behind a cutout of panes and then framing it with drapes made of a swatch of silk. She was surprised to hear Olivia's key in the lock in the early afternoon.

"Hi, Randy, you home?" Olivia called in.

Miranda found her in the kitchen, still in her coat, lighting the gas under some leftover coffee. She looked cold and miserable.

"You had a call," said Miranda, and she told Olivia about Rosamond Kessler. Olivia never took her eyes off the pot. She seemed almost not to be listening. When the coffee steamed she poured it into a mug and wrapped her fingers around it. Then she slumped on a stool. "I guess they're lowering the boom," she said softly.

"What do you mean?" Miranda felt

something like dread. Seeing the energy and drive go out of Olivia was like seeing her turn into another person.

"I mean, I think this is the way they give you the ax. Rosy Kessler is getting my desk and my office. I get hers, only hers is very near the door. Neither of us has tenure. One of us has to go. The department is thinning out, as Alistair puts it. One of us is about to be sacked and I guess now we know who."

"But Alistair is your friend." Miranda insisted.

"Which hasn't anything to do with it." Olivia looked at her for the first time. Her eyes were red-rimmed and clouded. "Anyway, was he a friend? He was something. Today I'm not sure of anything, including where our next nickels will come from."

"But you've got the magazine," said Miranda.

"Ha," Olivia said without mirth. "My dear daughter, free-lance editing does not keep us in chopped chuck."

"So this is what Townsend wouldn't tell me," Miranda remembered out loud.

"Yeah. This was the big secret. She picked it up snooping in Alistair's closets."

"But you can get another job," said Miranda.

"In this day and age, my dear, when schools are cutting back as never before? I've the chance of a Popsicle in hell."

"You have so many friends and you're famous," Miranda shouted.

Another miserable "ha" from Olivia. "Articles, some TV spots, a bunch of lectures. I was hot stuff for a while, but this town gets bored fast. Issues are changing, the times change, and the question at hand is rent money."

Miranda couldn't think of anything else to say. She went back to her room, sat down on her bed, and considered this new and incredible turn of events in their lives. She picked Dinah up and thought that only a few hours ago the most important trouble she could imagine was a talk with Olivia about Dinah. Dinah was very far from Olivia's concerns right now. And Dinah seemed very far from anything of importance in real life.

As Miranda looked at the doll an idea started to root and then bloom in her mind. She pushed it out of her thoughts only to have it sneak back. She grabbed Dinah and forced herself to walk her through one of her favorite dramas, but the story bogged down and she realized she wasn't enjoying it. She thought then of calling Mildred. But Mrs. Munson said that Mildred was out. She sat down in the living room and tried to read. Nothing came of it.

This being the first day of the New Year, decisions and resolutions were in order. She made one. It was the one she'd tried to push out of her mind for the last few hours, along with Lydia Fenwick's words, "worth a small fortune" and "cash her in for a bundle." She wrote her resolution down on a piece of blue notepaper to make it official. Then she dressed Dinah in her most beautiful gown, a complicated plum velvet with lace collar and sleeves, a bustle, and jet buttons. She put Dinah in one

shopping bag and her packed steamer trunk in another. Then she stripped the shelves of all their dollhouse trappings so that they became once again plain closet shelves. This kept her busy for the rest of the afternoon. She and Olivia ate an early supper of party leftovers and went to bed. Miranda wanted to get a good night's sleep so that she would be ready for the following day. The last day of her vacation was going to be very busy indeed.

14

It wasn't difficult to find Graham's Antiquities. Miranda had checked the address carefully in the Yellow Pages and even telephoned the shop to make certain it would be open. The telephone call had had to be made in whispers because Olivia was still at home and Miranda didn't want her to know anything. "I'm going to the library" was all she had said when she stood at the door in her jacket holding a shopping bag in each hand.

"I probably won't be here when you get back," Olivia had said, looking up from her typewriter. "So I'll call you later in the afternoon . . . and, oh, Randy . . ."

Miranda's heart had stopped for a moment, and she had tried to squeeze the shopping bags behind her back.

"We still haven't had our talk. Please don't think I've forgotten."

She thinks I *want* the talk, Miranda realized as she walked east toward the sign on Mr. Graham's shop. Boy, does she ever not understand me.

The shop was just what she had imagined. Down three steps, through a clean window divided into many panes, an arrangement of beautiful furniture so delightful to behold that anyone, Miranda thought, would want to settle down right there in the window and call it home. There was a wing chair by a mantelpiece with footstool drawn up, two majolica cats watching out of yellow eyes, a cheerful hearth rug, a wigstand topped by a bowl of holly. Miranda's breath began to steam up the window. She could hardly tear herself away.

As she opened the door a bell rang someplace. Through aisles of carefully arranged furniture, bric-a-brac, and china, there appeared one of the thinnest and longest men Miranda had ever seen. He created the same effect as the furniture in his shop, costly and elegant, only not nearly as cheerful. The furniture glowed with polish and wax, while he seemed burnished by health and care. He frowned as he approached Miranda.

"Can I help you?" he asked in a sharp and not very pleasant voice.

"Yes, uh." Miranda wanted to turn and run. His brief icy-blue look made her keenly aware of the stains on her pea jacket, the missing button, the frayed sneakers, and the ratty-looking shopping bags. She knew she was an eyesore in this shop. "Are you Mr. Graham?"

"I am."

"You collect old dolls?"

"Antique," he glared. "What is this about?"

"It's about Dinah," said Miranda, bending to take the doll out of her shopping bag. "I've come to sell her to you."

She could feel Mr. Graham bristling in front of her, but she didn't look at him until she had Dinah firmly in hand. "She's in perfect condition and she has a very large original wardrobe." She held Dinah up for inspection and for a fraction of a second she was certain she caught an expression of surprise and delight in the long narrow face above her. But it was quickly gone, replaced by a look of sneering disinterest.

"That? What is that?"

"Dinah. She's very rare and special."

"My dear child, she's a dime-a-dozen copy. The Japanese are turning them out now. Very clever they are, too."

"She is not a copy." Miranda's voice went up unsteadily. "Look, she's signed." She pulled the collar down to show him Dinah's inscribed nape.

"Mmmmm." He bent forward and held a pair of glasses up to his wintery eyes. "Yes, I see, but they copy that too." Suddenly he took Dinah out of her hands and strode to the light from a Tiffany lamp, where he turned her around several times, inspecting her very carefully. "Well, she's a well-made copy. I could perhaps make an offer."

"Jeremy." A voice called from the back of the shop and was soon followed by a woman who had to be Mr. Graham's sister. She was equally long and thin and had the same cold eyes (though not the same bald head). Thin blond hair framed her narrow face.

"Look at this child's clever copy, Sybil," he said, holding the doll up. "I was just about to offer her something for it. Even if it is a copy, it's a rather nice one."

Their eyes met for a moment, and Sybil gave Miranda the same summing-up look her brother had, missing no bases: stains on jacket, lost button, sneakers. "Yes, it's a sweet thing. Good copy, or fair. I've seen a few of these."

"She's no copy." Miranda grabbed Dinah back. "She was up in an attic for fifty years with her clothes and everything. You're trying to trick me."

Both Grahams drew together and glared

at Miranda, who stepped back a pace under the double-barreled superior gaze.

"I am an expert. Whoever told you fifty years was mistaken. The doll is a clever copy."

"What about this?" Miranda pulled the steamer trunk from her shopping bag and opened it. "What about the clothes and the trunk?"

Mr. Graham looked briefly at the trunk. "The trunk is real and the clothes are old. They aren't worth very much, but they're worth more than the doll. Fifteen dollars for the clothes and another five for the doll is my offer. Really, I don't think you can do better."

Miranda felt as if she were choking. She put Dinah back in one shopping bag and dumped the trunk and clothes in the other.

"That's rather a lot of money for a little girl," Miss Graham piped up. "I shouldn't think you'd often see that much."

"It's nothing," said Miranda, "nothing but peanuts and you know it."

"You are a very rude little girl," said Mr.

Graham. "I wonder, in fact, how you came by a doll like that." His tone was threatening.

"*A doll like what?*" Miranda shouted. "A *copy?* You said she was just a copy."

"Now just a minute." He seemed suddenly ruffled in his tweedy feathers. "Just a minute. My sister and I thought you were interested in a little pocket money. Perhaps I should have another look at her."

"Not on your life." Miranda walked toward the door.

"My brother may have been hasty." Miss Graham followed her. "We certainly would like to rethink the offer. Another look at the doll would be helpful and then we can discuss . . ."

But Miranda had opened the door and shut it with a violence that astonished her. "Finks," she said over her shoulder. She walked to the corner, cheeks stinging in the cold air, not knowing where to go next. She felt loaded with anger and energy. Those two thought she was some jerk in ragged clothes who'd either stolen Dinah or come upon her accidentally. She'd been treated, she knew, like an idiot just because she was a kid in a dirty pea jacket. She stood on the corner thinking of these things when the light turned, and she realized she didn't know where to go. Her anger turned to misery, and with a slow trudging step she went home.

15

Home was where she sat down and watched television without paying any attention until she realized it was growing dark and she was getting hungry. In the kitchen Miranda found Olivia, who had come in so quietly she didn't realize it. Olivia was sitting at the table in her coat, looking at the toaster.

"I didn't hear you come in," Miranda said.

"Oh." Olivia didn't turn around.

Miranda was alarmed. She had never seen Olivia like this before. She seemed to be a study in defeat. "Mother, Olivia, what happened?"

Olivia turned slowly and blinked. "I've been sacked. I know I told you I thought I would be, but the actual event in living color kind of knocks the wind out of you. Pardon my blues."

"Is it because of money?"

"That's fifty per cent of it. The rest is my damaged ego."

"How much do we have in the bank?"

"My, but you're the practical one."

"I mean it, Olivia, what do we have and

what do we need and what can we make?"

"We?" Olivia's brows raised. "Excuse me, but what on earth are your money-making plans?"

"I have something of value to sell."

"Miranda love, your eyeglasses and blue jeans may be precious to you, but on today's market . . ." she shrugged.

"I'm talking about Dinah and her clothes."

"Oooooh, Dinah," Olivia drew in her breath. "Yes, of course, your doll, your secret playmate. I would never ask you to part with her."

"But I tried to sell her today," said Miranda. "I took her to some stuck-up antique dealer who wanted to gyp me."

Olivia's eyes opened very wide. "You what?"

Miranda, who had been exploding with her untold adventure, described it for Olivia from beginning to end. Along the way she told her about Mrs. Small and Dusty and Mildred.

When she had finished Olivia sat back

and stared unbelievingly. "Is this *my* kid?" She smiled. "Is this quiet, shy, never-opens-her-mouth Miranda?"

"The Blimp and the Lump," Miranda added.

Olivia laughed. "My, but you've gotten around town with that little doll of yours." Her face grew serious and she paused. "While we're on the subject, how come the big-secret stuff? You really made me look like a jerk."

Miranda pressed her lips together and stared at the floor.

"Now don't clam up on me, Randy, not now when I really need a friend. Level with me."

"I know how you feel about girls playing with dolls, that's all," Miranda blurted, still looking at the floor. "I know you think it's role playing and stupid and I know how proud you were to tell people how I didn't play with them," she added softly.

There was a long silence. Olivia lowered her head and held it in both hands as if helping it to contain whatever thoughts were going on there. "I guess," she started slowly, "that I was forcing you into a way of behaving just as I had once been."

Miranda didn't say anything.

"I really was shoving you, wasn't I, Randy, and that's why you had to show me and rebel just as I once did."

"No," Miranda said. "It wasn't for that reason. I really loved playing with Dinah. It wasn't to hurt you. Really it wasn't." She was pleading.

"It was to prove to me that you are a free agent. Not something I can push around."

"That's not true," Miranda shouted. "I just loved to play with Dinah."

"Then why were you trying to sell her once you'd proved your point?" Olivia was relentless.

"To help out," Miranda said. "She's worth a lot. Remember what Lydia Fenwick said. You're going to lose your job and I wanted to bring in something for us, Olivia. You've been shelling out for me for years. All those groups I hated cost money. You don't get alimony or even child support. I know that and I know how you feel about it. A lot of people would have dumped me. I'm not pretty or smart. I'm no Towny."

Olivia's eyes were suddenly dimmed with what Miranda was horrified to realize were tears. She had never seen Olivia cry.

"Randy, you're my girl, and if I had a choice, you're the only girl I would ever have. Those groups were the way I had to do it to keep you with me. I wanted you with me. I'm sorry it was so awful for you. I didn't know that. You've got so much spirit and strength. I'm very proud of you."

"Then stop crying," Miranda said harshly. She got up and filled a glass with water and set it down in front of Olivia. The gloom in the kitchen was thick. A weeping, beaten Olivia was unreal for Miranda. Had she made up the other Olivia? "Listen." She put her hand on her mother's slumped shoulder. "I have to call somebody about the way Mr. Graham tried to trick me. I don't want him to get away with it."

While Olivia sat drinking her water, Miranda got Mrs. Small's card from her jacket and dialed the number. She told Mrs. Small what had happened.

Mrs. Small was outraged. Miranda could hear her bracelets banging, and Olivia even got up to listen in.

"That old horse thief," she hollered. "He knew perfectly well the doll was worth five hundred on today's market and another hundred for the clothes. He just thought he could bully you out of it because you're a kid. I'm going to give it to him. I'm calling him right now." She paused and lowered her voice a shade. "You went to him on my recommendation, so I'm responsible."

Oliva smiled and put a hand over her mouth.

"You stick by your telephone, kid," Mrs. Small bellowed. "That old swindler is gonna call you up and apologize."

Miranda hung up. Olivia ran out of the room with a war whoop. She flung off her coat and went into her bedroom. "I've got to hear this on the extension," she shouted. She was the old Olivia again. "Hey, Randy, that woman is terrific!"

When the phone rang Miranda and Olivia picked it up simultaneously.

"I wonder if I might speak with a Miss Perry," the man said.

"This is she."

"Ah, yes, my dear, Jeremy Graham here. I do wish you had told me you were a friend of Evie Small's, she's a very good client of ours. It is often so difficult to do a proper evaluation on anything that comes in off the street. One isn't really prepared and I did want to apologize for the misunderstanding. Of course your doll is quite authentic. Actually, I've taken the trouble to look her up. On today's market, she'd be worth in the neighborhood of five hundred."

"I see," said Miranda.

"And so if you would care to come in at

your convenience we . . . could discuss the sale again perhaps. That is, I should be happy to see you again and I hope you accept my apologies for the misunderstanding."

"The misunderstanding," said Miranda, "was because you thought I was a poor dumb kid and you could trick me. I accept the apology, but I wouldn't do business with you. I don't like labels stuck on me."

"As you wish," said Mr. Graham, and the phone went dead.

"Hallelujah," Olivia cried from the bedroom. She ran back to the kitchen and wrapped Miranda in a great hug. "That's my baby. You told him. No labels, not his and not your mother's. We really are on the same side, only I forgot where I stopped and you began. Now let's eat, I'm famished." She was the old Olivia all right.

In a few minutes pots were on the stove, water was boiling, party leftovers (still around) were being disguised and reborn. Olivia stirred and sampled. "By the way, I've decided to file a protest over my dis-

charge. Also, I'll try to go full time at the magazine. That should bring in shekels."

"And I am going to sell Dinah," said Miranda.

Olivia looked up. "Oh no you're not," she said. "I never want her to leave."

"Olivia, she's worth a lot."

"That's right. She's a symbol. The best one we've got."

"A symbol of what?" Miranda was exasperated. "Centuries of girls forced into patterns of play that restricted and stifled their potential?"

Olivia stopped stirring. She turned and put her hands on Miranda's shoulders. "A symbol of independence of thought, of the courage to follow one's bent in spite of propaganda, even popular and fashionable propaganda. Of not knuckling under. I need her around."

After Miranda had prepared for bed that night, she took out her school bag and some clothes for the morning. Then she unpacked Dinah and her steamer trunk. She put them on the bare shelf at the back of her closet. It occurred to her that she would not be playing secret games with Dinah anymore. Certainly she would bring her to Mildred's and take her out when Mildred came to visit, but the secret games had changed her real life so much that playing with Dinah would be different from now on. She got into bed and thought about telling Millie what had happened, about Mr. Graham and Mrs. Small,

about what would happen with Olivia's protest.

She sat up and turned on her light and looked at the small figure on the shelf of her closet. Amazing, a bit of cleverly molded bisque with glass eyes, through which Miranda Alexis (the Lump or the Blimp) Perry had grown to know herself and a few other things besides. Amazing.